To Carmen Da Costa, and the children & families

How th
Rainbow
Came to Be

to whom she devotes her efforts

May the rainbow of peace & justice always shine for all of you! Best wishes

Alma Flor Ada
Illustrations by Vivi Escrivá
Translated from the Spanish by Bernice Randall

Santillana

For Rita Esquivel, who has never forgotten she is a teacher, in gratitude for her work on behalf of all children and her example of determination and courage.

Santillana Publishing Co., Inc.
901 W. Walnut Street
Compton, CA 90220

94 95 96 97 98 8 7 6 5 4 3

Printed in the United States of America.

ISBN: 1-56014-221-9

Listen closely, for I'm going to tell you an old, old story about what the world was like before there was color. Long ago, Earth was all black and white, with various shades of gray. Nothing had any color: not the trees, not the rivers, not the flowers, not the sky, not the oceans. Even the butterflies went unnoticed, for they blended into the gray all around them.

Far, far away, Red, Blue, and Yellow, got together to talk about Earth.

"There can't be a planet without any color," Red declared.

"You're right. A gray planet is unthinkable," Yellow said.

"We must do something," Blue agreed.

But that's as far as their agreement went.

3

"We should paint Earth blue," said Blue.
"No, red!" shouted Red.
"No, yellow!" shrieked Yellow.

Each color thought it was
the only one that could
solve the problem.

4

Blue, the first one to visit the gray planet, said:
  "I'm the only color Earth needs. By turning the oceans and the rivers and the sky blue, I'll make it beautiful. Then, so there won't be any large, open places without color, I'll sprinkle blue on some berries and flowers."
When he was finished, Blue sat back and proudly inspected his work.

Next, Red arrived, saying:

"You can't do the job alone, Blue. A world that is all blue is very, very boring. It can't get along without me!"

So Red quickly took his brush to apples, strawberries, and lots of flowers. Before he was finished, he decided that a bird needed color too, so he turned the cardinal bright red. Then Red sat back and proudly inspected his work.

Finally, Yellow arrived, saying:

"Both of you would be lost without me. If you want your colors to shine, they need light."

So, Yellow reached up and gave color to the Sun. He was so pleased with the brightness that he sprinkled sunlight all over Earth. With quick brushstrokes, he then added color to many flowers, including goldenrods and marigolds and sunflowers.

Then Yellow sat back and proudly inspected his work.

With so much color, Earth took on a very different look. But there were still large patches of gray land.

Blue said: "Now that we've added color to so many things, the gray looks even sadder. But I can't paint the land blue, or it would blend right into the sky and oceans."

Yellow replied: "And I can't paint the land yellow, or it would look like part of the Sun."

The colors thought and thought. Finally Yellow asked Blue: "What would happen if we combined our colors?"

9

So they tried it. Blue and Yellow got together and
created Green for the hills and valleys.

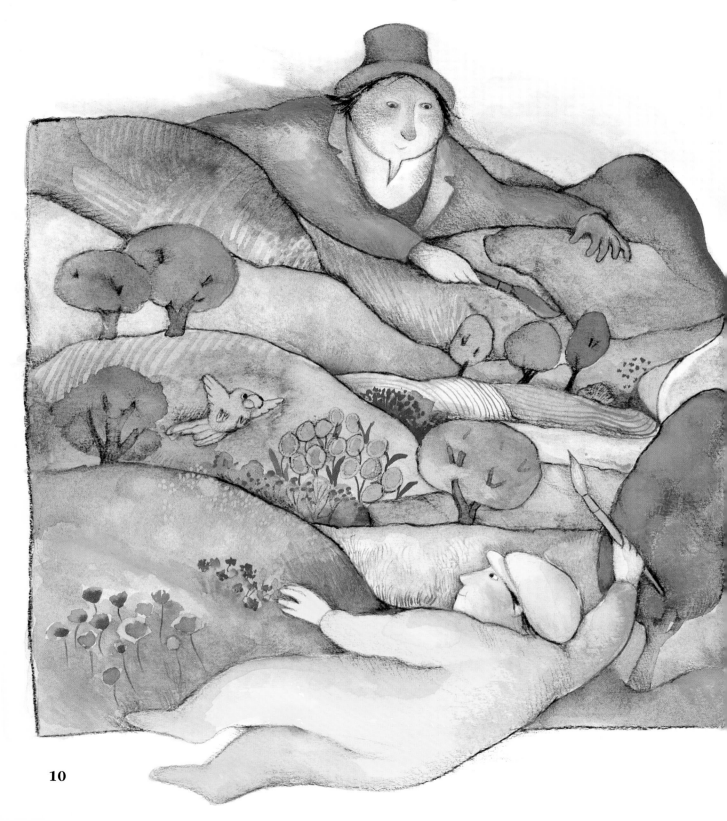

Then Blue turned to Red and said:
      "That's a good idea. Why don't we get together?"
In no time, there were several shades of Purple to give
color to grapes, violets, and sunsets
at the end
of certain
days.

Red liked the idea of creating new colors so much that he asked Yellow to join him.

Together they produced Orange, which was exactly the right color for oranges and many lovely flowers and birds.

Then Red joined the color black that he saw everywhere. That's how the land, the tree trunks, and many, many birds became Brown.

Red, Yellow and Blue sat back and admired their work. They were happy to have brought beauty to the gray planet.

They were also happy to have made new friends. So they smiled brightly.

13

Now each time it rains, the colors are happy because the rain gently washes the face of Earth, and makes them glow even brighter. To show their joy, they come together to create an enormous smile in the sky.
And, that is what we call a rainbow.